THIS CANDLEWICK BOOK BELONGS TO:

_____

_____

_____

_____

For Mum and Dad—I. B.

First U.S. paperback edition 1998

The Library of Congress has cataloged the hardcover edition as follows:

McBratney, Sam.
The dark at the top of the stairs / written by
Sam McBratney ; illustrated by Ivan Bates.—
1st U.S. ed.
Summary: Knowing that he must satisfy their
curiosity, an old mouse agrees to show three young
mice the "monster" and the top of the stairs.
ISBN 1-56402-640-X (hardcover)
[1. Mice—Fiction. 2. Curiosity—Fiction.]
I. Bates, Ivan, ill. II. Title.
PZ7.M47826Dar   1995
[E]—dc20   94-48921

ISBN 0-7636-0417-8 (paperback)

2 4 6 8 10 9 7 5 3 1

Printed in Hong Kong

This book was typeset in Veronan Bold.
The pictures were done in crayon pencil.

Candlewick Press
2067 Massachusetts Avenue
Cambridge, Massachusetts 02140

THE DARK AT THE TOP OF THE STAIRS

Sam McBratney

illustrated by Ivan Bates

CANDLEWICK PRESS
CAMBRIDGE, MASSACHUSETTS

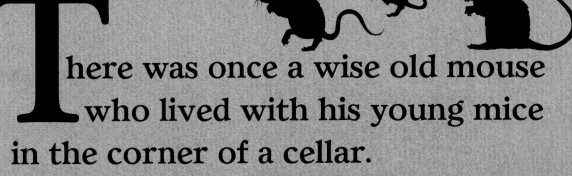

There was once a wise old mouse
who lived with his young mice
in the corner of a cellar.

Every day the old mouse liked to
do something interesting with his
young mice.

"What should we do tomorrow?"
he said one bedtime, for the young
mice were getting ready to sleep
and he wanted them to look
forward to the morning.

"I would like to see the dark at the top of the stairs," said a young mouse whose name was Cob.

"Me too," said his sister Hazel, snuggling into the warmth. "I want to see the dark at the top of the stairs."

"And so do I," said little Berry-Berry, the youngest of the three. "We've never been to the top of the big

dark stairs where the monster lives."

The old mouse thought for a while. It was true that he had not taken his young mice up the cellar stairs.

Then he said, "What about a walk
to the acorn tree in the garden?

Or a visit to your cousins in the
cornfield? We could even have
a swing on the seedheads
of the long grass."

"No," said Cob. "We want to see the dark at the top of the stairs."

"Or we'll climb up there on our own," said Hazel.

"And see the monster by ourselves!" cried little Berry-Berry.

The old mouse nodded as he made his young mice comfortable in their bed.

"Very well then, we will go there in the morning," he said.

He spoke as if he knew that sooner or later all young mice will try to see the dark at the top of the stairs.

In the morning, as early sunshine lit up the cobwebs in the corners of the cellar windows, they set out on their journey.

"Let's not talk about
the monster," whispered
Cob on the third step up.
"I won't mention it
if you don't mention it,"
whispered Hazel.
"I won't talk about the
monster either," laughed
little Berry-Berry, who
hadn't learned how to
whisper yet.

After seven steps, they stopped once more. There was excitement in their eyes, and the young mice hardly dared to look up, for they were closer now than they had ever been to the dark at the top of the stairs.

"I wonder if it's really, really real?" whispered Cob.

"You said you wouldn't talk about it," whispered Hazel.

"I hope the monster knows we're coming!" cried little Berry-Berry.

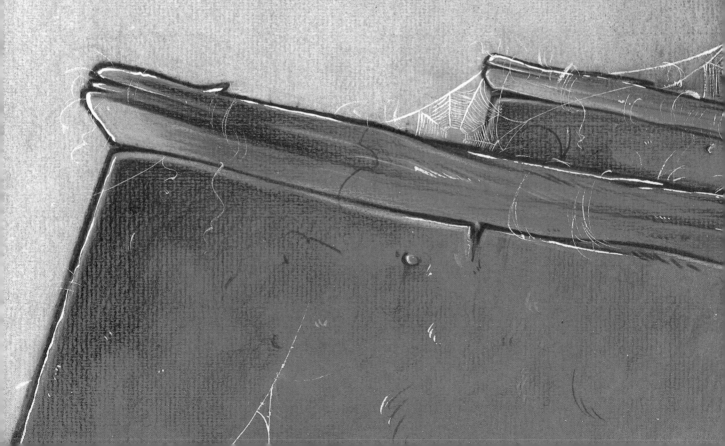

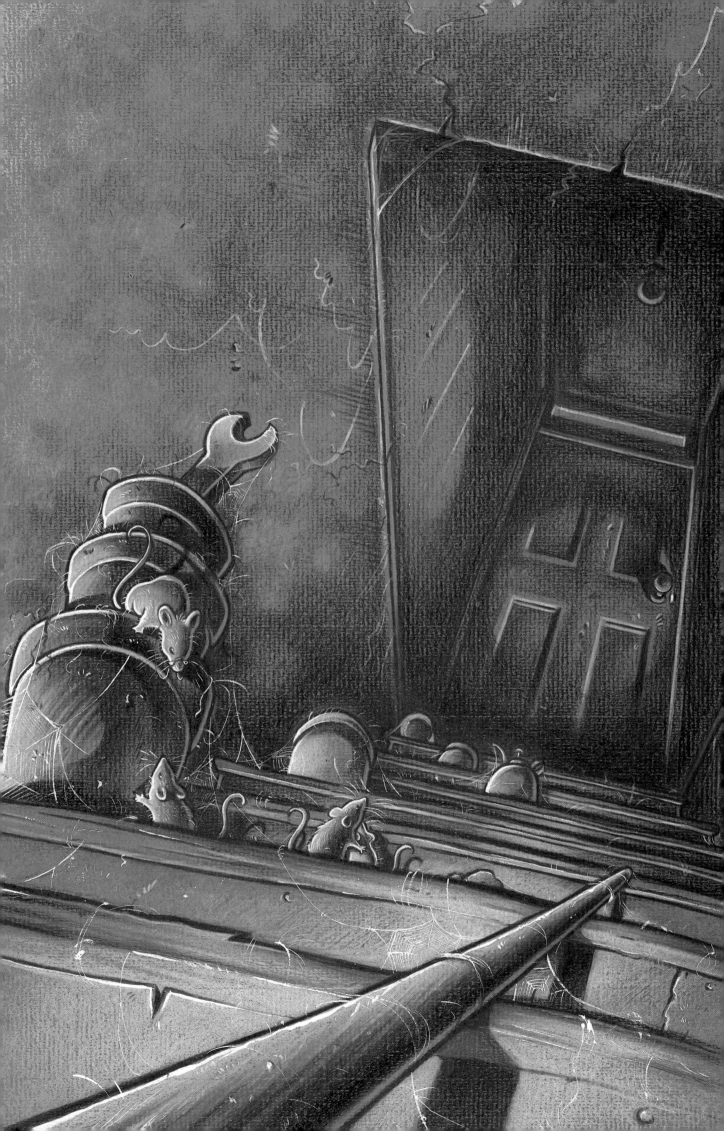

On the tenth step up, only two from the top, they paused once more. Hazel turned to the old mouse and whispered, "What is the monster like? Is it the most terrible thing anyone has ever seen?"

"We don't have far to go now," the old mouse said, and climbed the last two steps. After him came Hazel and Cob and finally little Berry-Berry, who said, "I don't see any monster at the top of the stairs."

Then something
happened.
The young mice
crept into a crack
of light . . .

They saw a monster shadow move
toward them as smoothly as a cloud,
and something breathed out softly
one strange word:

M E O W

The young mice did
not wait to say good-bye.
With wildly beating
hearts they went . . .

and tumble-thump

all the way to the bottom of the stairs, where they landed in a wriggle and a heap before making a dash for warm, safe, wonderful home.

At the end of the day the old mouse came to ask his young mice what they would like to do tomorrow.

"I would like to go to the acorn tree," said Cob.

"I would like to visit our cousins in the cornfield," said Hazel.

"I would like to swing backward and forward on the long grass!" said little Berry-Berry.

But none of them mentioned the dark at the top of the stairs.

Sam McBratney, the author of *Guess How Much I Love You,* observes that "there is so much talk these days about keeping children safe from danger that sometimes we go too far and forget that children must have the freedom to explore. The old mouse in this story knows that the inquisitiveness of young ones is matched only by their determination."

Ivan Bates says illustrating *The Dark at the Top of the Stairs,* his first picture book, was a challenge at times. "I spent so much time looking up stairs to get the perspective right that I ended up with a sore neck. And then I had to draw a lot of cobwebs, and since I'm not friendly with spiders, I was as scared as the mice."